Praise for How Dachshunds Came to Be

"A must-have for a primary school or public library...perfect for initiating meaningful discussions and exploring 'what if' questions."

— Marianne Stewart, Retired Early Childhood Educator

"Kizzie's tall tale is as much fun as low tide at the beach! While telling a delightful story, she weaves in the practice of leaving living creatures in their natural habitat...Kizzie gives voices to sea creatures rarely heard from...Scott's charming illustrations bring these creatures to life and help imaginations of all ages run wild with the dachshunds on the sand!"

— Laura Firth Markley, Beach Naturalist & Interpretive Exhibit /Researcher

"...Young children will be mesmerized by the sophisticated yet accessible language and metaphors. ...art work is gorgeous...warm-hearted story that will be a joy to read over and over! Can't wait to see this book on bookshelves everywhere!"

— Kim Votry, Author, *My Own Magic*

"A lovely little story with a big message of compassion and caring."

— Songbird Snow, Author

"This lovingly crafted story with an original and whimsical surprise at the end...is a must for every little child's book collection."

— Monda van Hollebeke, Author, Poet, & Literature college educator

"A delight to read aloud...These adorable dachshunds capture the little girl's heart and leap off the page to capture our hearts, too!"

— Edythe Ann Stromme, Co-founder & President Caucasus Children's Relief Fund (CCRF)

"This lovely tale will become a classic 'Read to me, Grammy!' book in our house."

— Freeda Lapos Babson, Author & Illustrator, *A Royal Buggy Garden*

"Brimming with the kindness of friends... a magical seaside tale!"

— Mary Kay Sneeringer, Owner Edmonds Bookshop

"...this whimsical touching fable models the values of compassion, collaboration, and love as caring pathways for creating understanding and empathy for others."

— Ellin Snow, MSW

How DACHSHUNDS Came To Be

A Tall Tale About a Short Long Dog

WRITTEN BY:
Kizzie Elizabeth Jones

ILLUSTRATED BY:
Scott Ward

nce upon a time,
long, long ago,
a little girl lived
by a magical sea.

She loved the sea
and the soft sand
and walked the
beach every day.

Whenever the outgoing tide pulled back the waves, the little girl gazed at colorful sea stars, anemones, mussels, and barnacles.

Sea foam left behind on the shore from the surf reminded her of petticoats sashaying in the salt wind.

She combed the beach for **friends-treasures** left by the sea. She discovered:

shells,

sand dollars,

4

and purple **hermit crabs** strewn
on the beach like discarded toys.

The little girl knelt and whispered to each,
"How special you are.
I wish you could come **home** with me."

5

Her **favorite friends** were a pod of gray humpback whales. The whales visited the Pacific Northwest twice each year. They migrated between their winter stay in the warm waters of the south and their summer stay in the cool waters of the north. How **happy** she was to see them and their newborn whale calves.

The pod played with her by blowing water up in the air. The spray caught the sunlight and made **shimmering rainbows.** Such fun!

How the little girl loved spending time with these friends. Sadly, she knew they **could not** go home with her.

One evening as the whales planned their migration north, they noticed the little girl was crying. They said, "You look sad. What's wrong?"

"Oh, dearest whales, you are my favorite friends. Yet, when you go out to sea, I go home alone. I long for friends who can stay. I don't think you can help me, but thank you for caring," and she blew them a kiss goodnight.

Later the pod gathered, joined by the many
sea creatures who also loved the little girl.
They all longed to help her **feel less lonely**.

At first, each of the sea creatures thought
a **companion** made in its own image
would be the **perfect friend** for her.

The **whales**, the smartest
of them all, reasoned,

"We want the new companion to be a
warm-blooded mammal like us, so it can
breathe fresh air just like the little girl."

The sand-colored
gooseneck barnacle said,

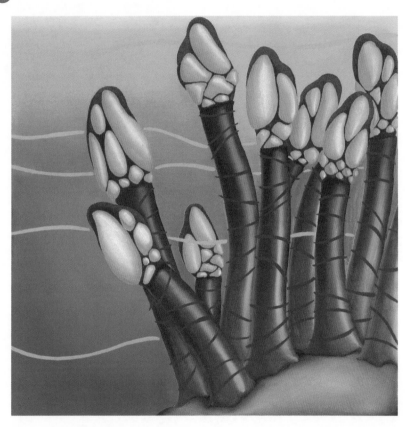

**"The companion needs to be like us
with a long nose to sniff out its food
and to snuggle with the little girl."**

The **gray seals** said,

"No! We want the new companion to be like us!
It needs a long sleek body,
to easily cuddle in the little girl's arms."

Soon the sea creatures realized **no single one** of them would be the right companion.

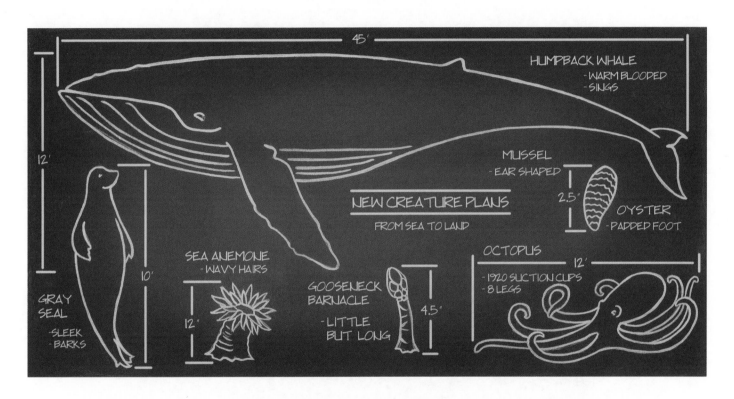

NEW CREATURE PLANS
FROM SEA TO LAND

45'

HUMPBACK WHALE
- WARM BLOODED
- SINGS

12'

MUSSEL
- EAR SHAPED

2.5'

OYSTER
- PADDED FOOT

GRAY SEAL
- SLEEK
- BARKS

10'

12'

SEA ANEMONE
- WAVY HAIRS

GOOSENECK BARNACLE
- LITTLE BUT LONG

4.5'

OCTOPUS
- 1,920 SUCTION CUPS
- 8 LEGS

12'

So, they asked themselves, "What if we could create a **completely new creature**, who mirrored our special qualities?"

The moon-shaped **anemones** asked,

"Could the new companion have soft wavy hairs for whiskers and eyelashes like us?"

"Why not give it ears shaped like us?" mused the **mussels.** They knew their shape would be pretty and practical, and offer protection from the sand and the wind.

The **sea grass** that moved so freely to and fro in the water suggested the companion have a tail. "It could wag back and forth to show how happy it was to be with the little girl."

The **Octopus** offered,

"I think the new companion should have eight legs
like me." The fish fretted and said, "Phooey!
We have no legs, why couldn't it be like us?"
After much talking, the group compromised on four
short legs—two in the front and two in the back.

"Because the companion will have to walk on legs," uttered the oysters,

"it will need something like us to cushion its steps— padded ends like our own inner bodies, protected by toenails like our super-thick shells."

As the story goes,
while the little girl slept,
her ocean friends, the magic of the sea,
and the power of love
created not **one**,
but **three**
new
companions!

When morning dawned, they rushed out of the sea
in green harnesses braided from sea cabbage.
One was **black** as the shadows in the depths
of the sea. Another was the **brown-red** shade
of the starfish. The third was
the *golden* color of an agate stone.
Each so **special**, so **beautiful**.

At once, they wagged their tails and ran
to the little girl, who scooped them up
in her arms. Long wet noses nuzzled into
her neck. She sat down on the sand as her
new friends frolicked in her lap.

The little girl
giggled
with
glee.

Floating on the waves, a **fun-loving
sea otter** offered the final gift—

"**Always** take time to **play**."

The whales breached in joy.
The waves **laughed** and **splashed** the rocks.

Now, as she walked the beach, her **three new friends** ran beside her.

She loved to watch their ears **flap and fly** in the wind.

Their **noses sniffed** out every scent in the fresh air and on the sandy beach.

27

After the little girl waved
goodbye to her dear whales
and said goodnight to her
sea friends, she guided her new
loving companions **home**.

As she hugged each one she said,
"I am **so happy**.
This is what I always wanted.

Best friends who can
play—and **stay**."

28

That was **exactly** what
the sea creatures
had intended.

And **that** is how
dachshunds came to be.

And they continue to
make people happy
to this very day.

the end

Biography

Kizzie Jones—Author

Kizzie Elizabeth Jones blends her love of dachshunds and her love of the ocean to create this whimsical tall tale to delight readers of all ages. Kizzie has been published in *Northwest Primetime, Chaplaincy Today, www.military.com*, and has been a first place non-fiction winner for Writers on the Sound.

This is Kizzie's first children's book. Kizzie and her ultimate hero, Thom, with their three dachshunds—Happy, Josie and Molly—live happily ever after in the seaside town of Edmonds, Washington.

www.kizziejones.com

Photo: Nancy Medwell, Hair Designer: Jody Wilson

Biography

Scott Ward—Illustrator

Scott Ward creates images reflecting the vitality of the human spirit while pushing the limits of the imagination. He has worked in advertising, clothing, graphics, interiors, theater, landscape, and murals.

Scott has always loved drawing, painting, and creating. How fun is that? Scott lives in Seattle.

www.scottwardart.com

This book is lovingly dedicated to

Edythe Ann Stromme,

the kindest of friends and the one who taught me how to be a friend.

Deep appreciation to my faithful "Writing Sisters," Monda van Hollebeke, Joanne Peterson, Reni Roxas, Julia Eulenberg, Andra Lawrence, Mimi Armstrong, & Edythe Stromme; enthusiastic publishing coach Emily Hill; creative illustrator Scott Ward, my Beloved Thom Wert who made 'once upon a time' a reality in my life, and our children and their families.

And gratitude to my parents, Kizzie and Carl Schleusing, who brought my first dachshund, Dagwood, into my life, which began a life long love of dachshunds. But, that is another story....
Kizzie Jones

To Ron and Pat—who let this goofy kid draw on his bedroom walls. Look at what happens.

Scott Ward

Made in the USA
Lexington, KY
08 December 2016